Transitioning

PRAISE FOR *STORYSHARES*

"One of the brightest innovators and game-changers in the education industry."
– Forbes

"Your success in applying research-validated practices to promote literacy serves as a valuable model for other organizations seeking to create evidence-based literacy programs."

- Library of Congress

"We need powerful social and educational innovation, and Storyshares is breaking new ground. The organization addresses critical problems facing our students and teachers. I am excited about the strategies it brings to the collective work of making sure every student has an equal chance in life."
– Teach For America

"Around the world, this is one of the up-and-coming trailblazers changing the landscape of literacy and education."
- International Literacy Association

"It's the perfect idea. There's really nothing like this. I mean wow, this will be a wonderful experience for young people."   - Andrea Davis Pinkney, Executive Director, Scholastic

"Reading for meaning opens opportunities for a lifetime of learning. Providing emerging readers with engaging texts that are designed to offer both challenges and support for each individual will improve their lives for years to come. Storyshares is a wonderful start."
- David Rose, Co-founder of CAST & UDL

Transitioning

Dean Gessie

STORYSHARES

Story Share, Inc.
New York. Boston. Philadelphia

Published in the United States by Story Share, Inc.

The characters and events in this book are fictitious. Any similarity to real persons, living or dead, is entirely coincidental.

Storyshares
Story Share, Inc.
24 N. Bryn Mawr Avenue #340
Bryn Mawr, PA 19010-3304
www.storyshares.org

Inspiring reading with a new kind of book.

Interest Level: Middle School
Grade Level Equivalent: 3.1

9798885979146

Book design by Storyshares

Printed in the United States of America

Storyshares Presents

1

"You pronounce it *mix*. Try it with me, children. *Mix* Rogers."

"Mix Rogers."

"Well done. Any questions?"

"Do you have a cold, Mx. Rogers?"

"No. I am feeling better than I have in a long time."

"Did you go to Disneyland?"

"No. I was absent for personal care."

"Your voice sounds different."

"Well," said Mx. Rogers, pointing at every student, "a voice is a unique instrument, isn't it?"

The children were confused, but flush with interest.

Serena said, "My dad has a tie like that."

Felix said, "I like your pants, Mx. Rogers. My mom says she wears the pants in the family, but she's not the only one. I have five pairs of pants!"

Mx. Rogers smiled and signaled for the children to gather round. "I have written a story," they said, "for story time."

The pupils moved obediently into an open semi-circle.

2

Mx. Rogers read from their iPad.

"Ellie the Eel had smaller fins than her brothers and sisters. Therefore, she might swim off course and lose sight of her direction. The other eels wanted to help, but they didn't know how. Nigel, the Most Unkind Eel, called her Aimless Ellie."

Sarah raised her hand immediately and said, "You shouldn't call people names."

Micah said, "We're all different."

Elijah said, "I use fins and a life vest in the pool next door. If Ellie were my friend, she could use my life vest and swim with all the rest."

Daniel said his dog had babies.

Felix said, "I wear pants and so do my brother and sister. Sometimes, my sister wears my pants when they don't fit me, anymore."

Mx. Rogers nodded affirmatively to each student and continued.

"Ellie the Eel became separated from her brothers and sisters. She was not strong enough to make the climb upstream. The other eels looked on with sadness. They wondered why Ellie was not the same as the rest of the group. *You can call yourself Ellie the Eel*, said Nigel the Most Unkind Eel, *but that doesn't make it true.*"

Eugene said, "Nigel is not very nice."

Rajeev asked, "Is Ellie all alone?"

Mx. Rogers said, "Yes and no."

Elijah said, "A life vest would be just the thing."

And Felix added, "I have a pair of pants just for Sunday, but nobody in my family goes to church. They're just-in-case pants."

Transitioning

3

Mx. Rogers continued their story. "Ellie the Eel was having a real identity crisis. She needed to know who she was. And she was prepared to ask anyone.

"Early the next day, she came upon a seahorse who just happened to be giving birth to his babies. Ellie introduced herself and asked, *can you tell me who I am?*

"Sammy the Seahorse answered: *well, that's not for me to say, but you certainly are an early bird.*

"*'I'm not a bird!* said Ellie the Eel. *I don't have feathers and I can't fly!* Nonetheless, Ellie knew that eels eat worms, just like some birds. It was all so confusing."

But Eugene's confusion was elsewhere. "Can boys have babies?" he said.

Mx. Rogers said, "Seahorse boys do."

Sabrina said, "Your voice sounds different, Mx. Rogers."

Eugene said, "My brother got kicked out of the choir because his voice changed."

Serena said, "I like your haircut, Mx. Rogers."

Mx. Rogers answered another question before continuing to read. "Yes. You can take her at her word. Ellie is not a bird."

Felix said, "Boys and girls both wear pants."

4

"Later that morning," continued Mx. Rogers, "Ellie the Eel met a spiny water flea who happened to be making babies all by themselves. *I'm asking everyone*, said Ellie. *Can you tell me who I am?*

"Scarlett the Spiny Water Flea said: *well, that's not for me to say, but you certainly are an eager beaver.*

"*I'm not a beaver!* said Ellie the Eel. *I don't cut down trees with my teeth!* But she knew that eels spend much of their time in water and some of their time on land, like beavers. It was all so confusing."

Daniel raised his hand and made an observation. "My puppies and the flea babies don't have a dad."

Mx. Rogers approved of Daniel's comment.

Serena said, "Beavers build homes in the water."

Daniel said, "Our puppies look the same, but they're really different."

Mx. Rogers answered a question. "Yes," they said. "You can take her at her word. Ellie is not a beaver."

And then the children found themselves in a game of remembering.

"She's not a seahorse," said Chanel.

"And she's not a bird," said Eugene.

"And she's not a flea," said Serena.

"And she's not a beaver," said Micah.

"And," said Felix, "she doesn't have a pair of pants!"

About The Author

Dean Gessie is a contributing author to the Storyshares library.

Transitioning

About The Publisher

Story Shares is a nonprofit focused on supporting the millions of teens and adults who struggle with reading by creating a new shelf in the library specifically for them. The ever-growing collection features content that is compelling and culturally relevant for teens and adults, yet still readable at a range of lower reading levels.

Story Shares generates content by engaging deeply with writers, bringing together a community to create this new kind of book. With more intriguing and approachable stories to choose from, the teens and adults who have fallen behind are improving their skills and beginning to discover the joy of reading. For more information, visit storyshares.org.

Easy to Read. Hard to Put Down.

Transitioning